The Binky Ba-ba Fairy

Written by
Heather Knickerbocker-Silva
Illustrated by Adrian Silva

dog ear
PUBLISHING

First published by Dog Ear Publishing
4010 W. 86th Street, Ste H
Indianapolis, IN 46268
www.dogearpublishing.net

ISBN: 1-59858-251-8

This book is printed on acid-free paper.

Printed in the United States of America

I would like to dedicate this book to my son.
Aiden, I wrote this book just for you and then decided to
share it with the world. Thank you for loving the Binky-
BaBa Fairy story enough to let her come get your precious
pacifiers and bottles. You are becoming a big boy. I am very
proud of the person you are becoming and I love you.

When I was a little baby I drank from a bottle and I had a pacifier.

When I got older Mommy said I was getting too old to drink my milk from a bottle and to suck on a pacifier.

AS 2006

I was very sad. I wanted to keep them.
They made me feel better.

Then my Mommy told me about the
BinkyBaBa Fairy.

When babies grow up and become big kids they pack up all of their bottles and pacifiers.

They leave the bottles and pacifiers
outside their door with a note to the
BinkyBaBa Fairy.

She flies in to collect the bottles and pacifiers. Then she leaves a big kid gift for you.

Then she takes the pacifiers and bottles to deliver them to all the new babies being born in the world.

AS 2006

When you wake up in the morning the package with the pacifier and bottles is gone. But you have a gift that is only for big kids.

For a little while I missed my bottle and pacifier. But now I drink my milk from a cup and I don't need my pacifier to make me feel better.

AS 2006

I like being a big kid. I get to do more things that I want to do. I help pick out my clothes and decide what I want to eat for snack.

I feel good that the BinkyBaBa Fairy delivered my pacifiers and bottles to the little babies who need them. They will take care of them until they are big kids too.

LaVergne, TN USA
11 November 2009
163729LV00002B